Hello, Family Members,

Learning to read is one of the most important accomplishments of early childhood. **Hello Reader!** books are designed to help children become skilled readers who like to read. Beginning readers learn to read by remembering frequently used words like "the," "is," and "and"; by using phonics skills to decode new words; and by interpreting picture and text clues. These books provide both the stories children enjoy and the structure they need to read fluently and independently. Here are suggestions for helping your child *before*, *during*, and *after* reading:

Before

- Look at the cover and pictures and have your child predict what the story is about.
- Read the story to your child.
- Encourage your child to chime in with familiar words and phrases.
- Echo read with your child by reading a line first and having your child read it after you do.

During

- Have your child think about a word he or she does not recognize right away. Provide hints such as "Let's see if we know the sounds" and "Have we read other words like this one?"
- Encourage your child to use phonics skills to sound out new words.
- Provide the word for your child when more assistance is needed so that he or she does not struggle and the experience of reading with you is a positive one.
- Encourage your child to have fun by reading with a lot of expression . . . like an actor!

After

- Have your child keep lists of interesting and favorite words.
- Encourage your child to read the books over and over again. Have him or her read to brothers, sisters, grandparents, and even teddy bears. Repeated readings develop confidence in young readers.
- Talk about the stories. Ask and answer questions. Share ideas about the funniest and most interesting characters and events in the stories.

I do hope that you and your child enjoy this book.

— Francie Alexander
Reading Specialist,
Scholastic's Learning Ventures

D0959308

For Leif, my little buddy
— K.H.

For Max and Mia
— C.P.

Go to scholastic.com for web site information on
Scholastic authors and illustrators.

No part of this publication may be reproduced, or stored in a retrieval system, or transmitted
in any form or by any means, electronic, mechanical, photocopying, recording, or otherwise,
without written permission of the publisher. For information regarding permission, write to
Scholastic Inc., Attention: Permissions Department, 555 Broadway, New York, NY 10012.

ISBN 0-439-31703-7

Copyright © 2001 by Nancy Hall, Inc.
All rights reserved. Published by Scholastic Inc.
SCHOLASTIC, HELLO READER, CARTWHEEL BOOKS, and associated logos
are trademarks and/or registered trademarks of Scholastic Inc.

Library of Congress Cataloging-in-Publication Data available

10 9 8 7 6 5 4 3 2   02 03 04 05
Printed in the U.S.A.   24
First printing, September 2001

Busy
Chipmunk

by Kirsten Hall
Illustrated by Cary Phillips

My First Hello Reader!
With Flash Cards

SCHOLASTIC INC.

New York   Toronto   London   Auckland   Sydney
Mexico City   New Delhi   Hong Kong

Busy chipmunk in the fall—

See him in a tree so tall.

Busy chipmunk in the sky—

See him in a tree so high.

Busy chipmunk on the ground—

See how many nuts he found?

Chipmunk needs more food to eat.

Chipmunk, look—

A winter flurry!

Chipmunk Sounds

Look at the pictures below.
Point to the pictures
that begin with the
same sound as:

Rhyme Time

Rhyming words sound alike. Point to the picture that rhymes with the word at the beginning of each row.

tall

eat

sky

see

Opposites

Opposites are words that mean completely different things. **Wet** and **dry** are opposites.

Look at the words below. In each row, point to the word that means the opposite of the first word.

tall	funny	big	short
in	out	above	down
lost	see	found	look
fast	slow	hurry	high

Animal Homes

Match each animal with its home.

Winter's Coming

Point to the things you would need in the winter.

Then point to the things you would not need.

How Many Nuts?

The chipmunk is counting nuts.

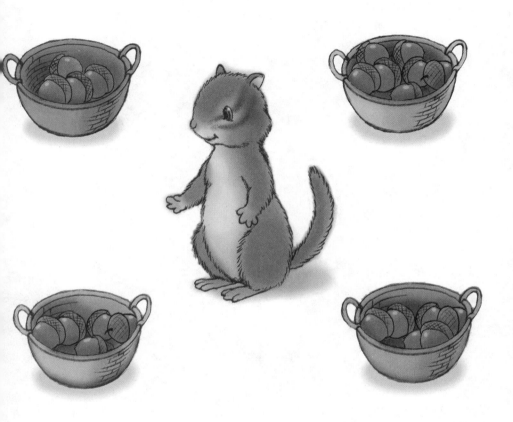

How many nuts are in the red basket?

Are there more nuts in the blue basket
or in the green basket?

Which basket has the most nuts in it?

Answers

p. 26: *(Chipmunk Sounds)*

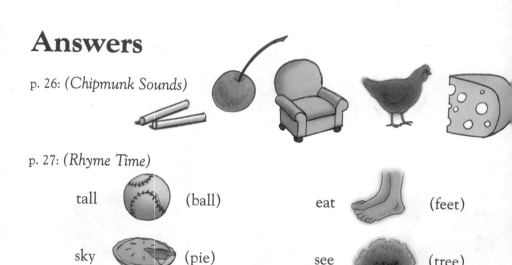

p. 27: *(Rhyme Time)*

tall ![ball] (ball)   eat ![feet] (feet)

sky ![pie] (pie)   see ![tree] (tree)

p. 28: *(Opposites)*

The opposite of *tall* is *short*.
The opposite of *in* is *out*.
The opposite of *lost* is *found*.
The opposite of *fast* is *slow*.

p. 29: *(Animal Homes)*

p. 30: *(Winter's Coming)*

In winter you would need: In winter you would not need:

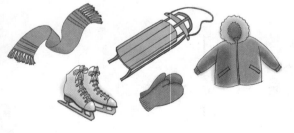   

p. 31: *(How Many Nuts?)*

There are four nuts in the red basket.
There are more nuts in the blue basket.
The yellow basket has the most nuts.